TO
TUCKER

Sludging through a Sewer

Also by Val Wilding

Toby Tucker: Keeping Sneaky Secrets

Toby Tucker: Dodging the Donkey Doo

Toby Tucker: Mucking about with Monkeys

Toby Tucker: Picking People's Pockets

Toby Tucker: Hogging all the Pig Swill

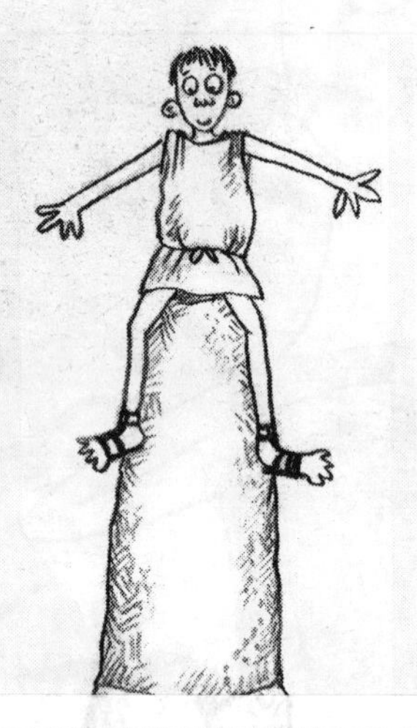

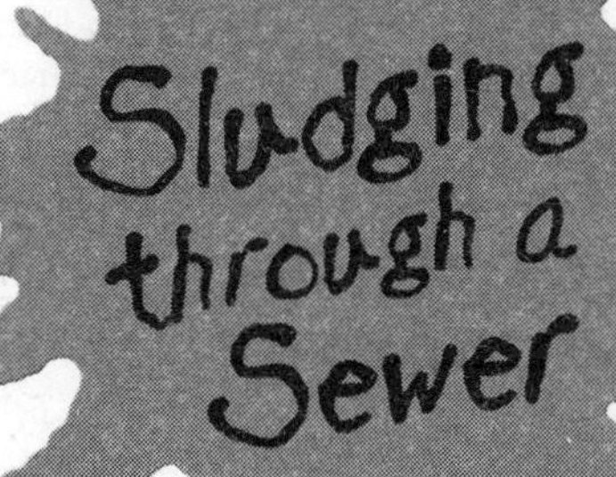

VAL WILDING

Illustrated by Michael Broad

EGMONT

For Gill and Mike,

and for Billie Bonkers, who shares my pink cloud.

EGMONT

We bring stories to life

Published in Great Britain 2007
by Egmont UK Limited
239 Kensington High Street, London W8 6SA

ISBN 978 1 4052 1838 2

1 3 5 7 9 10 8 6 4 2

A CIP catalogue record for this title is available
from the British Library

Printed and bound in Great Britain by the CPI Group

The Allen house, present day

Toby Tucker arrived home from school to find his two friends, Jake and Amber, waiting at the gate. 'I didn't know you were coming round,' he said. 'How did you get here so quickly?'

'Bikes,' said Jake, pointing to where they'd flung them behind the hedge.

The front door opened, and Toby's foster mother, Evie, looked out. 'Hello, you lot,' she said. 'Are you coming or going?'

Amber looked at Jake, who nodded. 'Coming, please, Mrs Allen!' Evie was known for always having something decent in the cake tin.

They all trooped in. Toby stopped dead when he saw Don, his foster father, surrounded by what looked like junk. 'Why are you packing up boxes?'

'Bits for the car boot sale,' said Don. 'Hiya, kids. Come round for one of Evie's sawdust sponges?'

'You'll get one on your head in a minute,' said Evie. 'Raspberry jam and all!' She cut the cake. 'Here, you lot, why don't you take it up to Toby's room . . .' She stopped when she saw his face. 'No, better have it here.'

Once they were eating, Jake asked Toby if he was putting anything in the car boot sale.

'Not likely,' said Toby. 'I haven't got much.'

Amber kicked Jake. 'Idiot,' she muttered.

'It's OK,' said Toby. 'Just about all I brought from the children's home was a wooden chest, my clothes and a few other bits. But Evie and Don have given me a CD player and lots of books and

all sorts of great stuff.' He grinned. 'I'm not taking any of that to a sale!'

Jake helped himself to a second slice of cake. 'What was in the wooden chest?'

Evie and Don glanced at each other.

'Just papers and stuff,' said Toby. 'Why did you come round, anyway?'

Amber said, 'Jake's got a new games thingy –'

'Console,' said Jake.

'– and it's got four controllers,' Amber continued, 'and we wondered if you want to come round tomorrow and play this brilliant game. You're a gladiator in Ancient Rome and –'

'Actually,' said Don, 'I really need Toby's help tomorrow. Can you make it Sunday?'

'We go to my nan's on Sundays,' said Jake. 'Maybe next Saturday?'

'Sure,' said Toby.

When the others had gone, he went up to his

room at the top of the house. Don followed a moment later. 'Sorry about that, lad, but I could use your help tomorrow. Evie's going to be busy stripping the bathroom door before we start tiling the walls.' He made a face. 'She won't let me do it – you know what a mess I made of the last one.'

Toby chuckled. There was a great big gouge in the airing cupboard door. Evie had gone ballistic!

He looked out of the window. 'Be nice to have a bike,' he said. 'I could get up later, because it wouldn't take so long to get to school, and I could come home earlier, and go out to play with my mates. I can't have them up here.'

Don looked round. When Toby came to live with them, he and Evie had only just moved in themselves. Weeks and weeks later, the walls were still covered in pink fairy paper.

'We will get it sorted, lad,' he said. 'Promise. Anyway, you get pocket money now. Why not start saving for a bike? You can pick nice ones up second-hand.'

Toby sat on the wooden chest that stood beneath the window. 'That would take too long,' he said. 'I don't have much left over at the end of the week – it's not worth saving.'

Don turned to go. 'Pennies add up,' he said, and checked his watch. 'Can you come down in half an hour and help me load the car?'

'Course,' said Toby. 'I'm going to . . . You know.' He reached down and patted the chest.

Don nodded. 'Hope you're successful. You've got two now, haven't you?'

Toby looked up at his pinboard. Two names were stuck up there. The first was 'Seti', the name of an Ancient Egyptian, and the second was 'Nikoleon', who was an Ancient Greek donkey driver.

Toby had been trying for ages to add a third name. Maybe this afternoon he'd be lucky. He waited for Don to go. His stomach squirmed with excitement as he knelt to open the chest. Nobody, not even the people at the children's home, had any idea of where Toby came from, or who he really was.

But the chest held a secret. He reached in and pulled out the framed photo of the elderly man with the gentle face. As always, a warm feeling came over him as he looked at it.

The mysterious message written in pencil on the back of the photo was sort of a clue, Toby supposed.

The paper in the chest is your family tree. I wonder which little baby tore it up, eh, Toby Tucker? Piece it together and you'll find out who you are and when you come from.

Gee.

When you come from! Not where!

That was the key to the chest's secret. That and the huge mound of torn paper inside. All he had to do was piece together a name, and the magic would begin again. He hoped!

But that was easier said than done. Toby settled on his tummy on the deep red carpet with a pile of paper before him. Propped on his elbows, he began sorting through them. Scraps of names from down the centuries – Toby's family tree. His ancestors.

'Jul,' he read. 'Lan . . . iko . . . Cel . . . veta . . . ' None of those seemed likely to go together. He remembered last time, when he'd tried a system. The idea was to choose just one piece – any

piece – then work through until you found the bit that matched. Toby closed his eyes and took a scrap at random.

'tus,' he read. 'Definitely the second part of a name, so the matching bit must have a capital letter.'

He found 'Sus', 'Laf' and 'Art', then 'Raf', 'Pol', and a tiny scrap with 'Ti' on it.

Useless. He pushed them aside, but the little one with 'Ti' stuck to his hand. He shook it off and it fluttered down beside 'tus'.

Toby caught his breath. Titus! Yes, that could be a name! He put the two pieces edge-to-edge,

rested his chin on his hands and waited. His heart pounded.

Just as before, a drawing began to appear, all by itself, beside the name. It was a drawing of a boy in a very worn tunic. And as soon as the picture was fully formed, it began to change again.

'It's me!' Toby whispered excitedly. He watched as the picture of himself changed back into the boy in the old tunic. It began to shimmer.

'Exactly like before,' Toby breathed, and waited. He knew that the shimmering light would grow, half as high as his room, then it would move towards him.

So it did. Look out, thought Toby, here comes

the eating-cold-jelly feeling. As the shimmering light passed over the length of his body to his toes, Toby turned his head.

'Yesss!' As he'd hoped, there in the window, in place of his wooden chest, was the boy in the picture – the boy in the old tunic. Toby knew all he had to do was get up and walk forward and the magic would begin. He'd be drawn towards the boy as if pulled by some powerful magnet. And then . . .

He jumped up. Too quickly.

'Uh, oh! Head rush!' He tottered dizzily across the floor. He was going to knock the boy over! 'Out of the way!' he shouted. But he was pulled in – there was nothing he could do to stop himself falling.

The room was spinning. Everything turned misty as he fell with a thump.

'Ooomph!' he said. 'My head! I feel peculiar. Why am I all wet? Where am I?' He screwed his eyes up for a second. '*Who* am I?'

His head cleared. 'Oh, Titus,' he said to himself. 'What's that revolting smell? You're going to be in trouble now!'

Rome, 118 AD

I didn't mean to drench the baby in fish sauce. It was an accident. Normally one of the other slaves goes to buy the liquamen, but his foot hurt, so Milla, the cook, sent me. Yes, everybody knows liquamen is the tastiest sauce in the world, but it does stink of rotten fish. And when a voice shouted, 'Out of the way!' I turned to see no one

there. It made me go dizzy. I somehow managed to trip over the guard dog and tip a whole jugful over the baby and into the household water supply. Whoops! Straight into the impluvium!

If the baby hadn't been left there, we slaves could have cleared it up before anybody knew anything about it. Now the entire family's furious with me! My master, Gaius Julius, said I must be the clumsiest slave there ever was. Why does he always pick on me? I'm not their only slave. They have about seventy at their country villa and farm. Here, there are twelve. I'm the youngest. I was born here. They called me Titus, which means 'saved', because that's what I was – saved. My mother died when I was born, but I was saved from being put out on to the hillside and exposed to die. What was I saved for, I ask myself? To be a slave, is the answer. That's all.

* * * * *

I'm worn out today. I stayed up later than anybody else last night except Damon, the doorkeeper.

Damon guards the house with our guard dog, Ferox. He sometimes makes offerings to Janus, the god of doorways, who has two heads. Damon can't keep one head awake, let alone two.

I had to scrub the whole impluvium, all by myself. Even when it looked all right, it still stunk. It took hours, and I had to be up at dawn

as usual, which was horrible, because I still don't feel quite normal after my dizzy spell yesterday. I'm not myself at all.

When I took young Marcus some water to wash his face in, he asked if there was anything fishy in it. Oh, ha. But when I went back downstairs I found Gaius Julius inspecting the impluvium.

'You did a good job, Titus,' he said. 'From now on, let's just have rainwater in here, eh?'

'Yes, master,' I said. Whew.

* * * * *

Marcus didn't go to school today, so we played hide-and-find. It's not that easy, because he's made up a rule that says when it's his turn to hide, he can move somewhere else if I get close. When it's my turn, I have to stay put and get caught.

Although my main tasks are running errands and delivering messages, I've also been Marcus's playmate ever since we were small. I'm not complaining! It's the one break I get from working.

This afternoon will be special. There'll be a dinner to celebrate Arion becoming a freedman! Arion is Greek, but he was captured in battle, brought to Rome and sold in the slave market.

Our master needed a secretary, and lots of Greeks read, write, do arithmetic and know poetry and stuff. So Arion came to live with us. Gaius Julius, who is a good master, gave him a regular peculium. Imagine having your own money to spend! But Arion saved hard, so he could buy his freedom. And today's the day!

Once Gaius Julius was up and dressed, he went into the tablinum, which is his office. He's a lawyer and people come to see him to get advice about the law, to borrow money, to get help in finding work, or just to pay their respects. Arion

makes notes of all these meetings. This is his last time as a slave!

All morning, Marcus, his scruffy sister, Drusilla, and older brother, Aulus, ran in and out, peeping at Arion and giggling. Julia didn't. She's fifteen, and much too ladylike these days. Quite uppity, too. Gaius Julius gave orders to Arion in a really bossy, snappy way, which is unusual. He and Arion smiled then. It was all for fun.

After lunch, Gaius Julius, Arion, Aulus and Marcus went to the baths. They took me along. Aurelia, my mistress, and Julia went this morning during the women's session. I don't think Drusilla's washed today.

First we stopped at the barber's in the forum while Gaius Julius and Arion were shaved. It looks so painful – scrape, scrape, scrape with a sharp razor. Arion got a nick on his neck, so the barber pressed some oil-soaked spider web and vinegar on it. I'd rather bleed.

It was so bo-o-ring waiting. I spent the time watching some of the street entertainers trying to earn a few coins from passers-by. There was a clumsy juggler who earned nothing at all, and a dreary poet who wandered round the forum reciting his terrible poems to anyone who'd listen. He got two coins from people who paid him to go away.

At last we headed for the baths, which wasn't

much fun either. Usually I help Marcus, but today I had to guard the clothes.

If you don't pay someone to guard your things, or have a slave to look after them, you could end up stark naked with nothing to wear!

The dinner for Arion was fun. Even the slaves enjoyed serving it because there weren't any guests, so everybody was relaxed. Arion was allowed to lie right next to our master!

I poured water over everyone's hands between courses, and wiped them with a soft cloth. I was so busy watching Arion being grand that I missed Aurelia's hands and poured it over her lapdog instead. Aurelia slapped me hard, and the dog got my ankle. I call it Snapdog!

When Arion had drunk quite a bit of wine, he made a speech. Most of the slaves had gone to the kitchen but I stayed behind the curtain in case anyone wanted anything. I'm glad I did, because what I heard has given me something to dream for.

Arion went on about how happy he'd been, and how he loves Rome and wants to stay. Gaius Julius interrupted and said he must live here as long as he likes. Arion said he'd be delighted to carry on doing his secretary job – for a proper wage! Everyone laughed. Then Arion said that now he's free, he's planning to do all the things he's longed to do – to see all the sights he's ever wanted to see. As he rambled on about pyramids, Sardinia, lakes and Creta, sea voyages and his Greek homeland, I suddenly realised how big the world is. I've only ever known Rome, and I've always thought how lucky I am to live here in the centre of the world. But there's so much more out there that a slave never sees.

I've thought a lot about Arion's speech. It made me realise that anything's possible. One day I could be free, just like him. One day I might visit other lands, and no one could stop me simply because they owned me. It would be up to me.

But how? I've no money. I don't own anything – except my box.

I keep my treasure box under my bed. Inside there's a curl of my mother's golden hair. Aurelia ordered it to be cut for me. My mother came from an island called Britannia, which is part of our Roman Empire. I wonder if all the Britons have golden hair. It must be a beautiful land. If I was free, I could see Britannia.

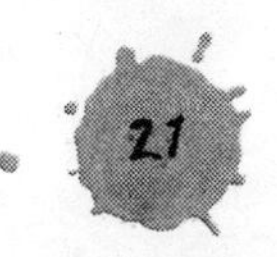

Today Julia's been dripping round the place moaning about next month's Saturnalia. The only people who'll listen to her are the slaves (her family get sick of her) and we're all thrilled that Saturnalia's come round again! It's a festival when school's closed, which pleases Marcus, and slaves have a holiday from work – and can't be punished! Best of all, slaves and masters change places for a day. Gaius Julius makes the whole family join in. Julia and Aulus hate it. Drusilla couldn't care less. Marcus hasn't taken part before but I bet he will this year.

And I bet I won't. Not after baby Flavia and the fish sauce.

*****

Praise the gods! Julia's getting married! That means she'll be moving out to live with her new husband, Quintus Didius Justus. No more wandering round nagging everyone. She does go on. Everything has to be peace and quiet and loveliness for Julia. If there's a leaf out of place in the

garden don't we know it.

Julia gets furious with Drusilla because she brings frogspawn in and messes up the pond. The gardeners get cross, too. When the tadpoles hatch Drusilla tries to stay awake all night and keep watch, because she knows Pero, the head gardener, whips them out whenever he gets a chance.

Today Julia ordered me to pick up a shrivelled lemon that had fallen from a tree. I knew what would happen. Pero tried to kick me for interfering. Sometimes you can't do right in this house, but one thing you daren't do is say no – not if you've got your head screwed on right. Nobody wants a beating, or to be sold off.

*****

Julia's driving everyone mad with her wedding talk. Because Maius and part of Junius are unlucky months for marriages, it's not till late Julius, for Juno's sake! How long must we put up with this? All day it's 'my white wool tunic, my orange veil,' and what flowers will decorate the house, and how she'll process to Quintus Didius's home with a boy lighting her way and three more boys escorting her. 'Blah blah blah . . . I'll put pieces of wool on the doorpost, and anoint them with oil blah blah and everyone will sing blah blah and I'll be carried over the threshold so I don't trip . . . that would truly be bad luck.' And then it's, 'And finally I'll say some very special words. Do you know what they are?' And everyone – even the slaves – shrieks, 'YES!' but she says them anyway: 'Where you are, there am I.'

Lucky old Quintus.

*****

I went to our usual baker today, but the fire for his oven had gone out. He was going crazy.

He was shouting at his slave even though it wasn't his fault – all he does is work the stones that grind the wheat.

I could have gone to another baker nearby, but Aurelia found a cockroach in his bread once, and won't let me go there any more. She'd know if I did. The bread's marked twice. Once to make it easy to break apart, and once underneath to show who made it. Aurelia says this one should have a picture of a cockroach on the bottom.

I went on a few streets to a baker I knew was all right. On the way, I saw a lady in brightly-coloured clothes. She wore armlets and bracelets from wrist to shoulder, three necklaces and the most enormous earrings. They had red glassy blobs on the ends, and swayed as she walked, like cherries in the wind.

As the lady stepped across the road, one of her earrings dropped into the gutter. Her slave, who was gazing at a soldier, didn't notice. I was about to pick it up when a man leading a mule pushed past. The mule's hoof flicked the earring against a stepping stone, and it bounced back against the kerb and disappeared into a hole.

The earring had gone. But where?

Another slave, Orban, and I took some dirty togas to the fuller's this afternoon. On the way, I pointed out one of those holes in the gutter. 'What's that, Orban?'

'Drains,' he said. 'Rainwater runs down there and washes mud and other rubbish into the

Cloaca Maxima.'

'Cloaca Maxima?'

'The Great Sewer,' he explained. 'It's like a

giant drain. Fresh water flows into it where it begins, then it goes underneath Rome, all the way to the River Tiber. On the way, all the drains from streets, buildings, toilets and bath houses empty muck and more water into it. Everything gets washed into the river and on to the sea.'

We reached the fuller's and dumped the dirty togas.

'Soon have those clean,' said the fuller. He will, too, but I don't like to think about what he cleans it with. Pee! And a mixture called fuller's earth.

I first heard about fuller's earth when I was five, and I thought it would be a good idea to wash Marcus's feet in earth – from the garden. He saw an earwig on his toe and screamed so loud that Snapdog crawled under a bush. When Aurelia told me to fetch her 'poor baby' out, it bit me.

On the way home, we passed the drain hole again. I wondered about that earring. What a waste.

* * * * *

Saturnalia today and nobody said I couldn't join in! They must have forgotten the fish sauce, even though Flavia's cradle still whiffs. First, Aurelia, Drusilla and Julia took five women slaves to the baths. I don't know what happened, but Julia came back in a filthy mood and said that's the last time she takes orders from a slave, and the sooner she goes to live with Quintus Didius and gets some respect, the better. Her father chose Quintus Didius for her. He's a bit weedy but, fortunately, Julia didn't hate him on sight, which might have something to do with the fact that he's both rich and powerful.

This afternoon, the men (and me and Marcus) went to the baths. Luckily, Marcus thought it was fun. He's just happy because there's no school for a week! We stripped off and Gaius Julius paid a servant to watch our clothes. Huh! I do it for nothing!

We rubbed perfumed oil into our bodies. Marcus said I usually smell of old sandals, but today I smell like a rose! I chased him outside to the palaestra. I wouldn't dare do that if it wasn't

Saturnalia. We did some exercises, then went for our baths. I went in the tepidarium first, then the hot, steamy caldarium. I finished off in the frigidarium. I wish I hadn't – it was icy!

While we dressed, I wondered how they heated the water. The servant asked Gaius Julius if he could show me. Marcus wanted to go, too, so that was all right.

There's a whole lot going on beneath the baths. There's a huge fire in a furnace, and all the hot air it makes goes under the floor and even up inside the walls. Pity the poor slaves who stoke the furnace. While we were there, one fainted.

I feel so clean. Bathing is brilliant, and I want to do it again. I can't wait for next year's Saturnalia.

Later on, we're having a posh dinner – served by the family!

* * * * *

Yesterday's dinner was the best! The nine most important slaves (not Arion!) had the places of honour. More couches and chairs were set up to one side. That's where I was.

Marcus served me! We had dormice roasted in honey, a dish of mushrooms and asparagus, snails in garlic and oil, oysters, then roast pig, roast chickens, roast deer, beans, turnips, and finally fruit, honey cakes, sweet pastries and prunes stuffed with nuts. Phew!

We had mulsum to drink. That's wine sweetened with honey, and it's the nicest thing I've ever drunk. It just slides down your throat. I had my cup filled five times, and when I got to bed I found mulsum had slid down the front of my tunic, too. Still, it doesn't show on brown.

I didn't touch the snails. I've been fattening them on milk for the last two days, and I almost

feel I know them.

Julia's face was like a brewing thunderstorm. Drusilla wandered in and out, not really with it. She's got some new kittens, and that's all she thinks about. Aulus made a complete mess of serving the oysters. He swore, and Milla ordered him back to the kitchen. 'Fetch more oysters, boy,' she said, 'and tell the cook that, by Great Ops, she's marvellous.'

Two of the spilled oysters were on my couch, so I flicked them off. Snapdog gobbled them up.

Later, I heard him being sick under a table. I suppose I'll have to clean that up tomorrow.

We all gave orders, but Orban whispered, 'Don't overdo it, Titus. Remember, tomorrow we'll be the slaves once more. Harsh words from us today would mean harsher treatment from them tomorrow.' After that, I said 'Thank you' a lot to Marcus!

Today everyone's quiet, but the family are back to normal. They're going out to dinner later, so we'll all feast on leftovers, and I'll play with the kittens in the garden.

* * * * *

After ten days serious house-cleaning, I had time to spare today, so I sat in the doorway chatting to Damon, and asked what would happen to something precious if it fell into the Cloaca Maxima.

'A sewer rat would get it,' he said, and pushed me aside as a litter drew up at the door.

When the entrance was quiet again, I was about to go back and ask Damon what he was on about – rats that eat jewels? – when Milla rushed up.

'Have you seen who's here?' she hissed. 'It's the mistress's mother! Go and buy some crab from the market. She's bound to want it. Hurry, Titus. Marcus is playing knucklebones with Aulus. He won't miss you if you're quick.'

It was lucky the fish seller had a crab. Aurelia's mother must be the only person in Rome who eats it. Most people loathe it.

When I got back, I discovered that Marcus and Aulus had gone to see a friend along the street. Nobody seemed to need me, so I slipped out again. I wanted to find the Cloaca Maxima – the sewer beneath the city. I thought perhaps the fuller might know where it was. He talks to everybody, and he seems to know everything. Perhaps he could tell me where to find it.

I raced downhill, turned a corner and ran – slap! – into Marcus. He grabbed Aulus's arm and we all fell against a bricklayer's handcart. The

bricklayer ignored Aulus and Marcus, but raised his fist at me.

Aulus glared. 'Where are you going?'

'I came to tell you your grandmother's visiting,' I lied. (All slaves lie a little. It saves trouble.)

'I see,' said Aulus. He led us, slowly, back to the house.

'We only came out because she turned up,' whispered Marcus. 'She pats me on the head!'

Lucky him, if that's all she does to his head. Last time she came I stepped on the hem of her palla and she thumped me on mine.

* * * * *

I've been so busy over the last few days I couldn't see the fuller till today. Luckily, it seems no one in this house can cope for a whole day without an afternoon snooze. Sometimes, if Milla drifts off, and I don't have much work, I have that time to myself.

Once Marcus began to snore, I left by the door in the garden wall and went to see if the

fuller knows where I can find an entrance to the Cloaca Maxima. If I could get in there, and if the rats hadn't found the earring, maybe I could.

He does! He reckons there are lots of manholes where you can climb down a ladder into the sewer. But there's a proper arched entrance, he says, not far from where we live on the Quirinal Hill. 'It's near the corner of the Forum of Augustus,' the fuller said. I know where that is.

I didn't have time to stand around. I knew

the sewer entrance wouldn't actually be in the Forum of Augustus, so I walked round outside. Not all the way round. At the back of the forum is a high wall, separating it from the Subura. That's the sort of place where you don't want to wander alone. It's full of robbers and cutpurses, and the people in the Subura are terribly poor.

I'd almost given up finding the sewer, when I caught a slight whiff of something like rotting cabbage. I followed my nose and found an open ditch, where clean water flowed towards a stone arch.

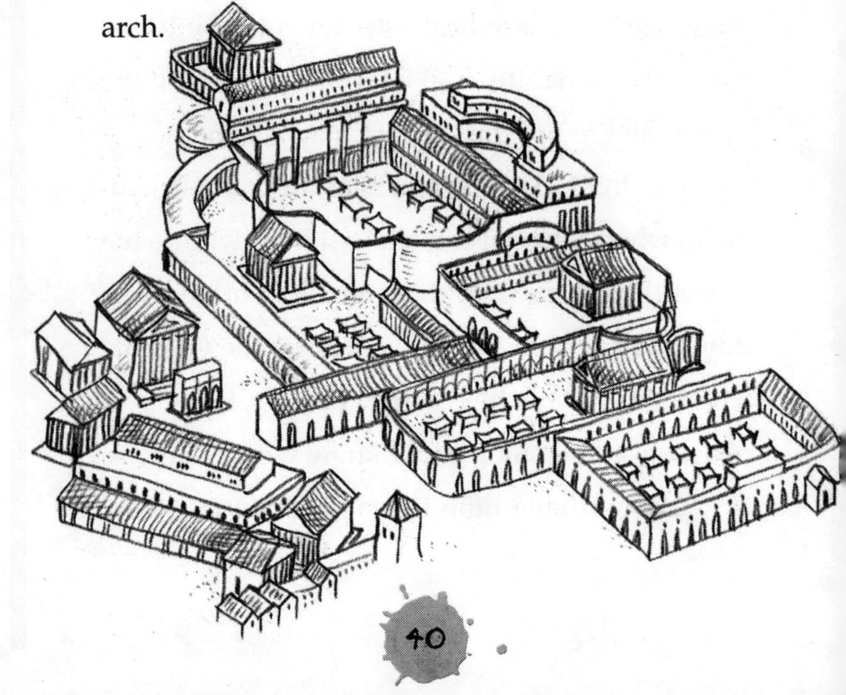

The smell came from the arch. I'd found the Cloaca Maxima! All I had to do now was watch out for rats. But not today. My shadow was long. It was getting late, so I took one last look into the archway. I wonder if the red earring's down there? Maybe there are other treasures in the Great Sewer. This could be the way to freedom – and Britannia!

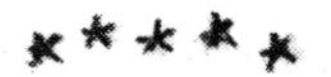

Today Aulus officially became a man, and no longer wears his bulla round his neck. He doesn't need protecting from evil spirits any more apparently! Julia will take hers off when she gets married. Perhaps her husband will protect her. Good luck to him!

In today's ceremony, Aulus offered his childhood clothes and bulla to the household gods at our lararium.

Till now, Aulus has worn the toga praetexta,

which has a purple stripe. From now on, he can wear the toga virilis – the white toga worn only by men who are proper Roman citizens. I wish him good luck. Whatever colour it is, it's a beast to put on.

The family have gone to the forum for more ceremonies to do with Aulus. There's a feast later, so we're all going frantic. The gardeners are trimming everything in sight, the floors are freshly scrubbed and everything's gleaming. No chance to get out. I have to help Milla.

Our toilet's in the kitchen, which is a pain, because I have to keep stopping work to flush it. On busy days Milla never has enough spare water, so I have to fetch it from the well. At least we've got our own toilet. It's nice to know that our sponge stick is used by just us, and not on any old stranger's bottom, like in the public toilets.

Am I tired this morning! When the guests arrived, I was helping Marcus get ready for yesterday's feast so at least I didn't have to wash and dry their feet. I hate doing that. The ticklish ones can suddenly send you flying.

The feast went on and on for hours. And being youngest, I got the yucky job. The vomitorium. There were so many courses that some people were full up halfway through. I stood in a side room holding a basin so they could make themselves sick and go back for more. Lucky Titus.

Tomorrow, Gaius Julius will be away, so it'll be a quiet day. While the family are having their afternoon snooze, I'll sneak out for another look at the sewer. But first I'll ask the other slaves about the rats. Suppose they're bigger than normal ones? And dangerous? I need to know.

* * * * *

I thought I'd never get away this afternoon. Marcus couldn't sleep because he'd eaten too many sea urchins in liquamen sauce (they were leftovers, and I wouldn't have touched them – even for money). Anyway, he was grumpy and tired, so he made me sing to him.

At last he dropped off, and I nipped through the garden door. There wasn't much chance of being spotted once I was outside, as most of our windows look inwards towards the garden. It's safer from burglars. Quiet, too. And we don't get street dust in the house.

Everywhere was hushed. Shops had closed for the afternoon, and there was hardly anyone about. At the sewer entrance, I slid carefully down the bank, so I didn't fall in the ditch. Then I edged sideways to the arch. The smell wasn't as strong as I'd expected, probably because here it was just fresh water running through the sewer.

I was nervous, because when I'd asked the others about sewer rats, they'd laughed and said things like, 'You don't want to get mixed up with them, Titus!' I peered into the arch and nearly jumped out of my sandals! Two people came out of the darkness towards me, wading through the water.

I leapt back, shot up the bank, and was sitting on the grass looking innocent when they appeared. They took no notice of me.

'Excuse me,' I said. 'Did you see any sewer rats down there?'

They laughed. 'Sewer rats don't stand a chance with us,' said one. 'We take them straight to the urban cohort.'

'What do they do with rats?' I asked. 'Eat them?'

I must have said something funny. The men could hardly climb the bank for laughing. I watched as they went to a little brick hut built against the archway. One reached into a crack between two bricks and took out a key. He opened the hut door and both men flung their boots inside. They wiped their hands on the grass and left.

If I had boots like theirs, I could go into the sewer. Before I left, I memorised the key's hiding place.

* * * * *

On the way home yesterday, I saw builders using a crane to

lift frieze blocks on to some columns. I made the mistake of telling Marcus, and this morning he told me to take him to see it.

'I'll get into trouble for not doing my work,' I said.

'Take me,' he ordered. That was that. I have to obey Marcus before any of the other slaves' orders. Never mind the trouble it gets me into with Milla.

He loved the crane, though.

I got fidgety, because I remembered I hadn't emptied the pots in the family's bedrooms (none of them ever use the kitchen toilet at night). I begged Marcus to come home. If we didn't get back before afternoon sleep time, I'd be in dead trouble. They'd be really thrilled to find full, smelly pots under their beds.

But Marcus stamped. 'I want to watch,' he said.

It's so unfair. I'd love to stamp my foot – on his – but, of course, I wouldn't dare. I got more and more edgy. I remembered that Drusilla's kittens had made their bed all smelly, so she'd told me to clean it up. If I didn't get back soon, there were going to be fifty different complaints flying around the house. All beginning with 'Tit-uuuuus!'

But if Marcus wants to do something, I'm stuck with it.

Then I had a brainwave. Milla had told me to fetch an amphora of olive oil, because she's running low. Those amphorae are so heavy that she lets me take the small handcart.

Marcus loves to ride on the cart, especially when I charge downhill and it bumps and leaps over

the cobbles. I sent him flying once – now I tie him on!

As soon as I suggested it, he said, 'What are we waiting for?' as if it was me who'd been hanging around.

I couldn't resist going past the sewer. Marcus moaned, 'Why are we going such a long way round?'

'Because it's quicker,' I said.

'Oh, all right,' he replied. (Honestly, I wonder about him sometimes.) 'But let's hurry. I want my ride.'

As we reached the sewer entrance, the two men were just about to go down. One saw me. 'Hallo,' he said. 'Rat-hunting again?' He hooted with laughter, until Marcus glared at him. Then he put his head down and shut up. He's only a slave, after all.

* * * * *

Marcus's paedagogus, the slave who takes him to school, is ill today. He must be really sick, because he's allowed to stay in bed. It doesn't matter what's wrong with me – I'm always working.

It's a real nuisance, because the paedagogus can't do his duty, which is to spend the morning at school with Marcus. And guess who gets the bo-o-oring job? Titus, that's who.

Marcus was cross before we left. He had such a great ride on the handcart yesterday that he wanted to go to school on it. I asked Aurelia, because he made me, and she said, 'Don't be stupid.' Marcus didn't believe she'd said that and got mad and threatened to have me whipped. Luckily his father heard him roaring, and told him not to be ridiculous. That shut Marcus up. His father's the paterfamilias – the head of the family. He holds power of life or death over his children, and they know it. He also holds power of life and death over me – and don't I know it!

We walked to school.

I stood at the back of the room while Marcus worked. The magister's voice droned on and on as he read from his scroll. I was nearly asleep on my feet by the time school finished. We went home and I fetched Marcus's lunch. Now that he's settled down for a sleep, I'll ask Milla if I can stretch my legs after all that standing.

Milla gave me some bread and cheese. 'Be back in one hour,' she said. I was pleased. Summer days are longer than winter ones, so each of the twelve daylight hours is longer, too!

By the time I reached the sewer, I'd wiped the last crumbs from my hands. There wasn't a soul around. I went to the hut and felt between the bricks for the key. There it was!

Some of the boots were wet. I guessed that

meant the sewer slaves had finished for the day. I took a dry pair, slithered halfway down the bank, and put them on.

The boots were cold and clammy, and felt disgusting, but I couldn't bear the thought of paddling in a sewer in bare feet. I slid further down the bank on my bottom until my feet were in the water. I didn't stop in time! The water came almost to my knees. It seemed quite clean, but of course I wasn't in the sewer yet.

There were drain holes further down where stuff poured in – stuff I didn't like to think about. Some of it was only rainwater, but some was sewage from public toilets – and from a few private ones, too.

I edged forward.

It felt slippery underfoot, so I was careful. It was all very well sitting in the stream, but I didn't fancy falling in the sewer. The smell was stronger now, and the damp air under the stone roof was chilly. I waded further in, not looking down in case I saw something nasty float past. Then I thought: Stupid fool! How will you find treasure unless you look down?

So I did. It wasn't bad – just twigs and dead bugs and bits of plants. No sewage yet. I examined the debris that collected against the sides wherever bits of stone stuck out and made a trap.

But I needed a stick to poke through it. And as I moved forward another few steps I realised I also needed a light. How could I have been so daft as to think I'd be able to see down here? I need a lamp.

The smell was getting to me. If it ponged here, I wondered how much worse the stink would be where a drain emptied into the sewer. I'm not giving up, though. No darkness, no stink will stop me treasure-hunting.

I made my way back to fresh air. Pulling the boots off was a struggle. They were sodden, and clung to my legs. It was lovely to wriggle my toes in the breeze.

I replaced the boots and key and raced home to a welcome from Milla in the form of a thump on the back of the head.

'Where've you been?' she snapped. 'Look at the colour of your legs!'

Marcus was out playing, so she told me to go and wash Drusilla's bedroom floor.

'Cats?' I said.

Milla shook her head. 'Spilled pot.'

Great.

* * * * *

Frosty-face sent for me today. She does the mistress's hair and make-up. If she messes up, Aurelia kicks her, and she's even worse than usual for the rest of the day.

Frosty-face wanted perfumed oil from a shop near the Roman Forum. 'You'll have to wait if it's not ready,' she said.

I didn't care! I hoped they'd say, 'You have to wait until sunset!' so I'd have a chance for a wander.

I was about to leave when I heard, 'Tit-uuuu-uss!' It was Aurelia. I ran to her. She hates being kept waiting.

'Take little Marcus with you,' she said. 'The poor dear's so bored. He's got no one to play with.'

That's because Drusilla saw a puppy running wild in the street and was off chasing after it, Aulus wasn't back from school, and Julia was sulking because nobody wanted to discuss hair styles for her marriage.

We hung around the Forum for ages waiting for Aurelia's oil, and Marcus got hot and cross.

Another month almost gone, and there's still nothing new in my treasure box.

*****

Hooray! The family's going away soon to their villa in the country while the house is being decorated. They'll be away for eight whole days! A new tile floor is to be laid in the atrium, and a mosaic border around the impluvium. A painter's coming to redecorate the triclinium walls. Whenever the family are away we have to have a big clean-up, but this time we won't start for a few days, because the workmen will make so much mess.

*****

They've gone! I love it while the family are away, even though I'm being worked as hard as usual. I have to help the gardeners redo the gravel paths. But we make as much noise as we like, and we go where we like. Aurelia's taken Frosty-face

with her, so that's one enemy out of the way.

I helped the mosaic artist this afternoon. It's really warm today, but cool and dim in the atrium.

Tomorrow, the garden work should be finished. Maybe I'll get down to the sewer.

* * * * *

Once everyone – Ferox and Damon included – was asleep after lunch today, I took the lantern from beside the front door, and hurried to the sewer. On the way, I broke off a piece of olive branch, and stripped off its dusty grey-green leaves. My poking stick!

It was so warm. The whole of Rome must

have been asleep! The only sounds were the odd dog barking and sometimes a baby's cry. The shops were shut for a couple of hours, before opening for the late afternoon and evening.

All was still and quiet round the sewer. I got some boots and dropped down the bank. The smell was strong today, probably because of the heat. The sewer looked different in the lantern's glow. Weird. And scary. I could see just so far, and then there was a wall of blackness that shifted as the lantern swung.

Don't waste time being scared, I told myself. If there was anything down there, I'd surely hear it.

I swung the lantern upwards. The tunnel was

two or three times as high as me. You could drive a cart down there!

Every time I found a clump of rubbish, I broke it up with my stick. I'd done this about ten times when I realised that if anything was caught up in the clump, it would sink when I pulled it all apart. I needed something to slide beneath the clump while I looked through it. Otherwise, it was arms in the water. Ugh.

I came home empty-handed. On the way, I stopped at a water fountain to clean up a bit before Milla got a whiff of me.

*****

I watched the painter for a while today. He's painting lemon trees, flowers and fruit on the walls. He wants to make it hard to tell where the garden ends and the triclinium begins. I think he's expecting a bit much there – I mean, the garden begins where the walls stop, doesn't it?

They're also going to paint the columns to look like marble.

I can't wait for everyone to drop off this afternoon. The lantern's full of oil, my poking stick's ready, and I've borrowed a spare tile from the floor layer.

I'm going to collect the meat from the butcher. On the way I'll try to work out whereabouts in the sewer that earring might have landed. Wouldn't a red jewel make a great start to my freedom fund?

Mercury's wings!! I've got an idea! If I start at the drain where the jewel disappeared, and count my steps to the sewer entrance, then next time I'm in the sewer, I'll walk that number of steps back underground.

Now this is getting exciting.

*****

By Jupiter!! What a day! When I went out, the city seemed fast asleep. I got my boots and went into the sewer. I had to walk two hundred and twenty-seven steps to get to where the earring drain was. I'd counted forty-four when I heard voices. The two slaves!

I turned to run back to the entrance, but my foot slipped on some rubble. I clamped my lips together as I fell so I wouldn't get a mouthful of anything disgusting, but some went up my nose. That was the least of my worries, because what stupid thing did I do? I dropped my lantern.

It was like the whole light of the world went out. I have never known such blackness. My heart thumped in my chest. I was too terrified to make a sound. Or so I thought.

Around a curve in the tunnel came a glow of light. I couldn't see who was there, but I heard them.

'What's that?'

'Dunno.'

'Listen – it's an animal.'

'Rats?'

'Rats don't whimper. Look, over there.'

'Careful! Might be a crocodile. They say people throw their pet crocodiles down sewers. They grow huge and –'

'Shut up. There's that cry again.'

I suddenly realised that the cries they heard were coming from me.

'Help me!' I called.

Strong arms pulled me up. They held me until we reached the sewer entrance, and beautiful warm sunshine. I flopped down on the bank, and spat and spat until my mouth was as dry as chalk.

'Thank you,' I said. Then I looked at my rescuer, whose bare legs were filthy with sludge from the sewer.

'Who are you?' I asked.

The man laughed. 'Just a couple of sewer rats,' he said. 'This is my son, Lucius. You a sewer rat, too?'

At last I knew what Damon meant when he said a sewer rat would get the earring. They weren't animals at all. They were people who searched the sewers for treasure, just like me.

'Yes,' I said proudly. 'I'm a sewer rat. But my lantern went out and I fell.' Not strictly true, but it would do.

'Here it is,' said the boy. 'Father trod on it when he picked you up.'

Thank you, gods. Imagine Damon's reaction if he found it missing! He'd kick me so hard I'd fly.

The lantern – and I – dried off on the way home. We both stunk, though. I told Milla I'd fallen over and landed in donkey droppings. She wouldn't let me eat until I'd washed in the fountain. Twice. She reckoned I still smelt after the first wash.

* * * * *

I didn't have much time today because the family are due back late afternoon. I put fresh blankets on the beds, and helped clear up the last of the workmen's mess. The mosaic artist is giving his floor a final polish, but the painter's not finished yet. The weather's so nice, though, the family will

probably eat in the garden triclinium.

I did find time to see the sewer rats. I know when to go, because they said they always go down at the same time, and have never been caught. I had a present for them – a jug of leftover wine. The jug was an old chipped pottery one, but the wine was good – the master's best.

'It's to say thank you,' I told them. They drank half of it straight off. Then they said I can go down with them a couple of times, till I get used to it.

Lucius showed me a ring he'd found yesterday, and part of a gold brooch they'd found today.

So there is treasure in the sewer.

The family came back three days ago, so there's been no chance to go sewer-ratting. There've been bags to unpack, and Marcus had to be taken to the baths, and for a haircut. And who gets the job of taking all the dirty clothes to the fuller? Tit-uuuus!

Today I spent all morning going back and forth collecting clean clothes, delivering mes-sages, shopping – and planning my next sewer visit.

But Marcus finds it hard to sleep in the after-noons now the weather's warmer. I tried fanning him with ostrich feathers. I thought he'd dropped off once, so I stopped, but he growled, 'Keep going.' He tossed and turned, then decided he wanted to play dice in the garden.

I don't want to play dice. I want to go sewer-ratting!

At lunch today I didn't put as much water as usual in Marcus's wine, and I kept his cup well topped up. When Aurelia sent him for his nap, he dropped off instantly and snored loud enough to wake a sleeping volcano.

In a quarter of an hour I was at the sewer, where Lucius and his father were ready to go.

'If you find anything, you can keep it,' Lucius said. 'Just don't expect us to share our finds with you.'

I waded behind them, hanging on to their boat, which used to belong to the engineer who checks the sewers for leaks. They borrowed it once (without asking) and never took it back. 'Why don't you keep your boots?' asked Lucius.

'You're joking,' I said. 'Where would a house slave hide something like that?' Truth is, I don't feel it's right to keep them. That's stealing. And I'd really be for it if I was found out. We don't steal in our household. I borrow things quite often, though.

Boots were the last thing on my mind as I hurried home. I made my first find today! It's a small ivory pin. 'Probably belonged to some little rich girl,' said Lucius. 'To keep her hair up.'

When I got back, Marcus spoiled my excitement by screeching at me so loudly that everybody soon knew I'd disappeared and left him all alone and he'd been scared when he woke up and his pot was full because I'd forgotten to empty it. That's a lie. I emptied it this morning. He'd drunk too much, and filled it up again.

'If you go out tomorrow,' he said, 'I'm coming with you.'

'Your mother won't let you,' I told him.

'But you won't tell her,' he said. 'Will you?'

Oh, wonderful.

I'm not going anywhere for a while. I'll wait till Marcus forgets about me sneaking out.

* * * * *

An amazing day! Gaius Julius took Marcus to the Circus Maximus to see chariot-racing for the first time. I went with them! The Emperor was there! I've never seen him before. I thought he'd be huge, but he's the same size as other men. The charioteers paraded through the streets, then entered the Circus. We all jumped up and cheered for our teams. I was green and Marcus was blue. I hoped blue would win, then he'd be in a good mood.

The chariots lined up, the Emperor dropped a white cloth and they were off! The noise was unbelievable!

Marcus changed teams with every race. He went for red, white and blue, but never green. He said he didn't want the same team as a slave. After that, I secretly changed to reds.

There were twenty-four races. Gaius Julius kept wandering off to talk to his friends. Once or

twice he bought us snacks. When the day was over, the greens were judged the winners. The crowd went wild, and so did Marcus. Tough.

On the way home, I asked Marcus to ask his father if I could speak to him. Gaius Julius heard me. 'What is it, Titus?'

'Thank you for taking me to the Circus

Maximus,' I said. 'It was . . . wonderful.'

He looked puzzled. 'It was not a gift to you, Titus,' he said. 'I took you as company for Marcus while I spent time with my friends.'

And that was that.

Marcus fell asleep instantly this afternoon. I thought yesterday must have worn him out. That and the tantrum he threw this morning when he had to have his feet measured for new sandals for Julia's wedding.

I slipped out and hurried to the sewer. I'd just slithered halfway down the bank, when something rolled past me, shrieking, and fell – splash! – into the stream.

Marcus!

The little beast followed me! He only pretended to fall asleep!

I pulled him out of

the water.

'I'm all wet!' he screamed at me. I'd like to have screamed back, 'Whose fault is that?', but it's more than my life's worth to aggravate one of the family when they're in a rage.

'Ssh,' I pleaded.

'Don't tell me to shush!' he roared. 'Dry me!'

I'd like to have dried him with a piece of pumice stone from Mount Vesuvius! I stripped off his tunic and gave him mine. Then I put his on. It was too small and, being wet, wouldn't slide over my skin.

That cheered him up.

'Why have you got a lantern?' Marcus asked suddenly. He looked at the boots, the archway and my face, which was getting hotter and hotter. He's guessed, I thought.

But before Marcus could speak, there was a

splashing sound from the tunnel entrance as Lucius and his dad appeared in their boat.

'Hello! Two sewer rats today, eh?'

I pretended not to know them. They looked at me oddly. I was dressed in a snow-white tunic – well, half-dressed – and Marcus was wearing a brown tunic, fit for a slave. How could they know he was my master's son? Behind Marcus's back, I shook my head, hoping they'd understand what I was trying to say. Don't speak to me! Thankfully, they went.

Marcus folded his arms. 'You're going down there, aren't you?' he said. 'That's why you asked the other slaves about sewer rats. You go looking for them.'

I didn't dare speak. If I admitted it, Gaius Julius would know by dinner time. I could get a beating – or even be sold.

Marcus took a deep breath. 'If you can go in there, so can I,' he said. 'Take me.'

'What about the rats?' I said. 'They're huge –

bigger than me, even.' Well, it was true.

'Don't lie,' said Marcus. 'Take me!'

I laughed. 'How could I take you down there?' I scoffed. 'You saw – you need a boat. I haven't got a boat.'

Marcus smiled sweetly. 'I have.'

Apollo's eyeballs!! What have I let myself in for? Marcus is absolutely dead set on a trip down the sewer. If I won't take him, he says, he'll tell Aurelia I pushed him in the stream. Little liar. Today he keeps eyeing my feet and saying loudly, 'Pooh! Titus, have you trodden in something?'

The little brat keeps on and on at me. The truth is, his boat would be very useful – if only it was mine and not his. I could go much further down the sewer and visit all the places where stuff flows in. That's where I'll find treasure.

Perhaps it won't hurt to take him just once. He'll hate it when he gets in there. This boy's used to baths, and perfumed oils and flower gardens. He won't last more than a few heartbeats in the sewer.

I'm collecting some material Aurelia's ordered for her wedding outfit this afternoon. I'll take Marcus then. We'll just float about a bit where the stream enters the sewer. Perhaps he'll be so pleased that he'll let me borrow his boat again.

*****

Marcus told Pero the gardener he wanted to sit in his boat and play sailors. Pero got it out and put it under a tree, in full view of the pond where Drusilla likes hunting for bugs and frogs and things – and leaving them in stupid places.

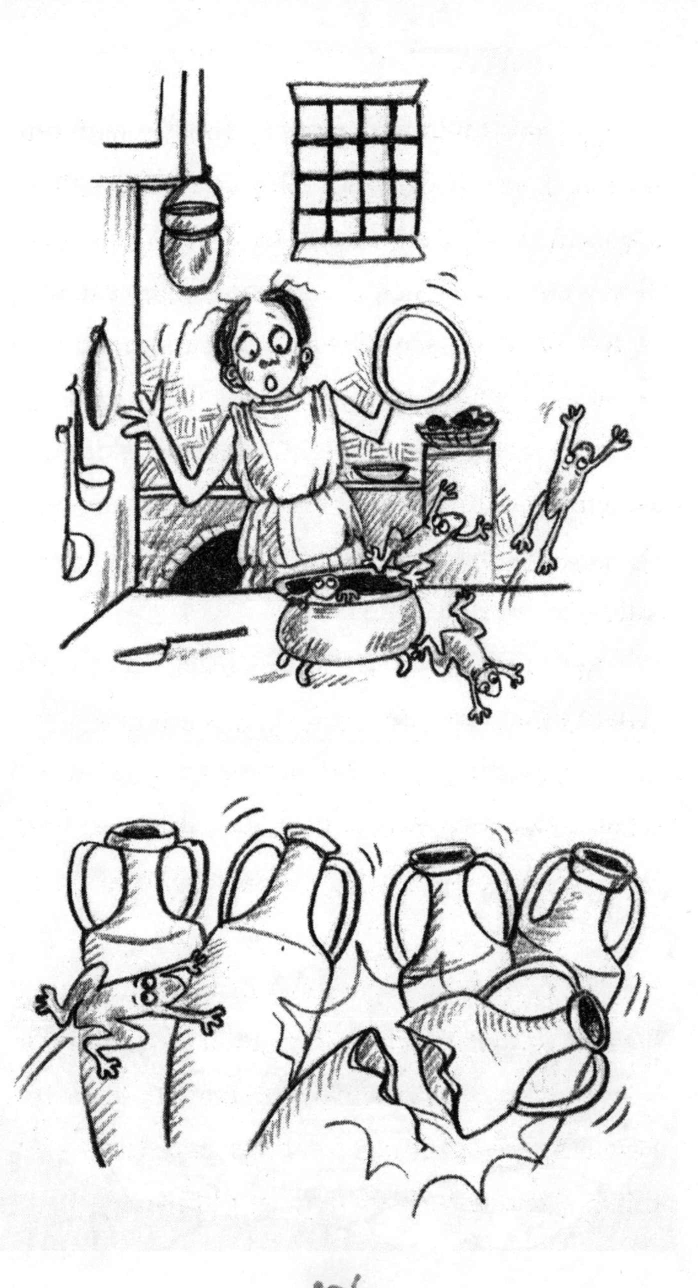

Marcus told me to drag the boat – with him in it – down the gravel path to near the garden door. He graciously carried the oar. When I said that wasn't much help, he got angry. 'I'm carrying it for you!' he screeched. 'What more do you want?'

His bellowing brought Snapdog skittering down the path, heading straight for my ankles. I nipped behind Marcus and waited for him to calm the horrible little beast.

'Off to Mother,' he told it. And off it went. That boy can handle dogs!

'Look, Marcus,' I said, 'if we're taking this, I'll need help, please. If I drag it, it'll be so noisy

bumping over stones and cart ruts, that people will notice us.'

'All right,' Marcus said. 'Just this once.'

So now the boat's sitting there, waiting for the family to go and lie down, and the slaves to have their lunch. Soon, we'll carry it (I hope) down the hill, and launch it on the stream.

Marcus asked where the stream comes from. I told him it was probably brought in by aqueduct.

Hurry up, everyone. Go to sleep!

* * * * *

I wish I could roll back time and still be in the garden with Marcus. I wish I'd never said I'd take him on the stream. I wish I'd never let him persuade me to go 'just a little way' into the sewer. I wish . . . Oh, what's the point? I wish I was dead. I probably soon will be, because there's no way to hide what I've done.

We launched the boat and bobbed into the sewer. We had no light, so I told Marcus we could only go a little way.

'A bit further,' he said.

Then it happened. The boat bumped against the side, and I pushed at the wall with the oar, to shove off again. 'We're going back now,' I said, firmly.

'We're not!' said Marcus. He grabbed the oar. We fumbled, and it fell into the water. I threw myself across him, grabbing for the oar, but the boat tipped dangerously. Marcus screamed, and I threw myself to the other side. We plunged backwards. Suddenly, I felt the most almighty crack as my head hit the wall, and then . . . nothing . . .

The next thing I knew was the sound of fast running water, and a thin wail. The wail was coming from Marcus, and the water . . .

The boat was speeding downhill, faster and faster. Terror gripped my guts as I realised we were hurtling, in utter blackness, towards the river. I can't swim. I was going to drown. Worse than that – I was going to drown my master's son.

I clutched Marcus with one hand, and gripped the boat with the other.

The boat was flung this way and that by the current, bouncing us off the walls. Faster still. Then . . . light ahead . . . a low arch . . . flashes of sun on water . . . Marcus screamed and clutched me as we shot into the light and down, down . . .

Splash! We were on the river! I've walked along the Tiber's banks often enough. I never dreamt I'd be floating on it – away from Rome.

Marcus got to his knees, sobbing. 'Keep still!' I snapped. Me – telling him what to do! But I was afraid we'd capsize. I slumped quietly for a few moments, trying to get my wits back. I ran my hand over the egg on the back of my head. No blood. My knuckles were raw and bleeding where we'd bashed into the sewer walls. I trailed them in the water. It soothed them.

We were out of the city now, being carried through open countryside. Without an oar (thanks, Marcus) we couldn't reach the bank. Marcus told me to shout to passing boatmen, but I was afraid to.

'We'll sort this out ourselves,' I said. The fewer people who know about it, the better, as far as I'm concerned. I felt sure we'd float towards the bank at some time, then I could grab an overhanging branch.

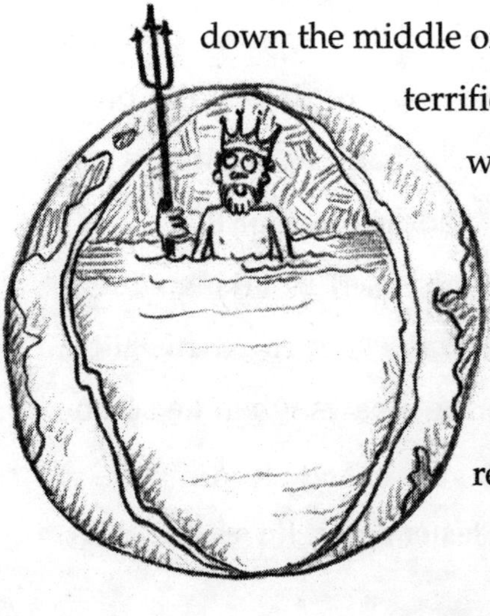

But we didn't. The current took us down the middle of the river. Now I was terrified we'd float all the way down the Tiber to Ostia and be swept out to sea. I silently prayed to Neptune, god of water, to return us to land.

I've heard about the

sea. It's called the Mare Mediterraneum, which means the sea in the middle of the earth. It's quite big, I think, and I don't want to go there.

The river widened and grew sluggish. I carefully knelt and used my hands as paddles to try to steer us towards the bank. 'You could help,' I told Marcus.

'I'm tired,' he whined.

It was time for plain speaking. 'I don't want to scare you,' I said, 'but if you don't help, we'll drift out to sea and be gobbled up by monsters of the deep.'

That shifted him.

Roofs shone in the distance. It was the port, Ostia. We had to get to the bank before it was too late. 'Paddle!' I cried. 'Paddle for your life!'

Poor Marcus was not used to taking orders from a slave, but he was so terrified his little hands went like Snapdog's paws when he scrabbles at doors.

The water moved faster again. It was hopeless.

We'd never reach safety on our own. I spotted a figure downriver. 'That fisherman!' I yelled. 'As we get near, yell as loud as you can.'

'What shall I yell?' the fool asked.

I took a deep breath. 'He-e-elp!' I screeched.

The fisherman looked up, saw us, and jumped into the water. As we drew near, I stretched out my poking stick towards him.

We were about to shoot past, when the fisherman threw his net over us and pulled us towards

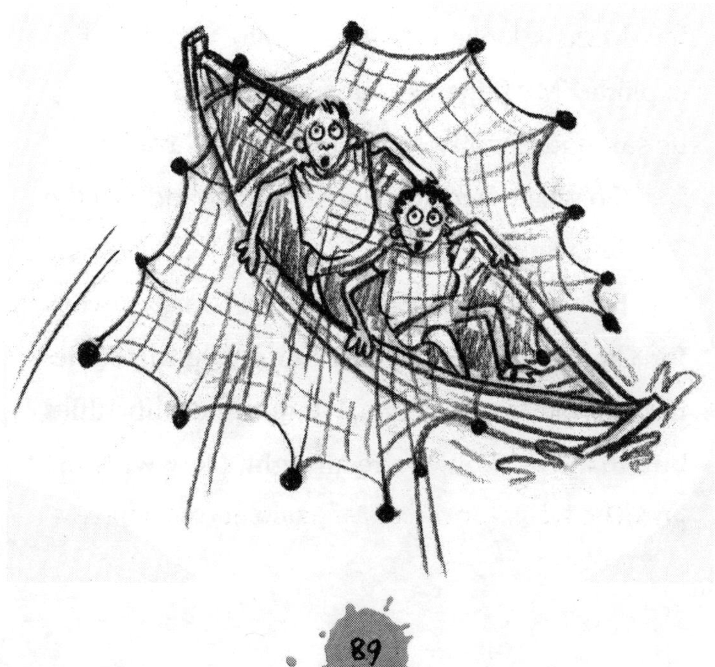

him. He reached out and grabbed my stick.

Moments later, we were on the bank, the boat was drifting towards open sea, and Marcus was grizzling, 'I'm wet again.'

The fisherman pulled off his wet sandals, then sniffed suspiciously. He tracked down the source of the smell – his hands. I slid my poking stick into the water before he realised where the pong had come from.

He turned to us. 'Are you runaways? Runaway slaves?'

Marcus looked as if his brain was about to explode. 'My father is Gaius Julius Felix of Rome,' he said indignantly, 'and Titus is my slave.'

'So what were you doing in the middle of the Tiber, scaring the fish?'

Before Marcus could answer, I said, 'I work for Gaius Julius Felix, and I'm delivering something important for him. We got into difficulties but, thanks to you, we're all right. Now we must go.'

I took Marcus's hand and we walked away, dripping.

'You lied,' Marcus said accusingly. 'You're not delivering anything for Father.'

'I am,' I said grimly. 'I'm delivering you.'

Because that's the most urgent thing in the world. I have to return Marcus to his father. And then I must take the consequences.

It seemed sensible to walk into Ostia to find

some food, and maybe get a ride on a cart going to Rome. Or even a boat – not that I particularly wanted to go on the river again.

I felt inside my tunic top. The money for Aurelia's material was still there, so we weren't in danger of starving. But I must be careful only to use it when absolutely necessary. I'll remember everything I spend so I can account for it. I don't want to be accused of theft, as well as . . . as . . . kidnapping, carelessness, disobedience, deceitfulness, lying . . .

Ostia is much smaller than Rome. It's quiet, too – until you get to the harbour!

Officials on the dock yelled, 'Clear off!' One eyed us suspiciously, then strode across and tipped up our chins. I know what he was looking for – slave collars. Probably thought we were runaways. We certainly look the part. Anyway, he was disappointed.

Gaius Julius trusts his slaves not to run away and none of us ever have. That's why we don't wear collars.

Marcus kept moaning about being empty. 'If you'd just get me home,' he grumbled, 'I could have my dinner.'

Always thinking of himself! I bought stewed vegetables and a chunk of sausage from the thermopolium.

People usually carry their own knife and spoon if they're eating out, but we hadn't got one. I borrowed one but Marcus was so hungry he just put his face to his bowl and flipped the food straight in. We ate in the doorway of an import company. It was easy to tell what they traded in because their mosaic showed a hunting dog being imported by ship. It might be from Britannia. Maybe my mother came on a ship like that.

When the company owner turned up, I leapt aside, pulling Marcus with me before we got kicked out. The man folded his arms and looked at us. I said, 'Sorry, we lost our boat and we're tired.'

'Where are you from?' he asked.

'Rome!' we said.

'Then you have a long journey in front of you,' he said. 'Almost fifteen miles.'

Fifteen! We won't make it home today, that's certain. Marcus's face was a picture. Before he started shrieking at me, I pointed to a ship coming in, and asked the man if he thought we could get a ride on it, if it was going to Rome.

He laughed. 'That ship's a sea-going vessel. She'll have travelled nigh on a hundred miles today, as the crow flies. The Tiber's not deep enough for ships like that.'

As we didn't want to go to sea, and we weren't crows, that wasn't much help.

'Sorry, boys,' said the man. 'But she'll unload on to barges. You might get a lift on one of those, though you'd be quicker walking.'

We went to the nearest barge, which was being loaded with sacks of grain. I asked Marcus to let me do the talking.

'Excuse me,' I said to the bargeman. 'Our boat capsized. Could you give my brother and me

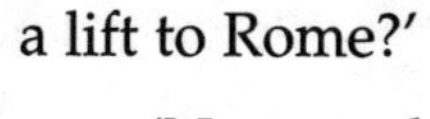

a lift to Rome?'

'Not at this time of night,' he said. 'Hey!' he shouted to Marcus, who was talking to a vicious-looking, slobbery dog. 'Be careful! She's dangerous!'

I wasn't worried. I know Marcus and dogs.

'By the gods!' said the bargeman. He couldn't believe his dog wasn't eating Marcus. He told me he was going upriver a bit, to moor for the night. 'You'd better stay in town,' he said. 'Barge people don't like strangers. That's why we have guard dogs.'

Just at that moment, his own guard dog was enjoying a tummy-tickle from Marcus. 'Yes, I see,' I said with a straight face. 'Come on, Marcus.' I led him away.

'You lied again,' he said. 'And you insulted me. Brother to a slave? Pah!'

I could have punched him. I bit my lip and took a deep breath. 'When that barge ties up for the night,' I said, 'the owner's bound to go to a tavern for some beer and food. You get the dog to let us aboard, then we'll hide among the sacks and sleep.'

We waited in the bushes alongside the tow-path and watched our bed – we hoped – glide slowly through the water, towed by oxen.

* * * * *

Thanks to my dog-tamer, we're aboard, and we'll have a night's sleep. Right now, Marcus is sleeping as deeply if he was on a bed of feathers. Poor kid's exhausted. Tomorrow we start our journey. Marcus's journey home. And my journey to . . . trouble.

We slept too late. I woke to the sound of oxen stamping as the bargeman harnessed them. I shook Marcus. 'Wake up!'

'Don't tell me what to –' he began, then looked wildly around.

'Sh!' I said. 'Let's creep away.'

I'd forgotten the rotten dog. She ran at us, jumped up at Marcus and licked his face. Then she glared at me, her lip curling. 'Grrrr!'

The bargeman looked round and bellowed when he saw us. 'Seize 'em!'

We ran! The dog bounded after us. No, not after us. After me. But Marcus grabbed her collar and shouted, 'Go!' I took off. When I looked back, the bargeman was about to grab Marcus, but he let go of the dog, shouted, 'Sit!' and pelted after me.

'Kill 'im,' bawled the man. But the dog sat looking at him as if he was barmy. The last we saw of them was the man shaking his fist – at the dog.

We had breakfast of crusty fresh-baked bread and walnuts, and water from a fountain. I washed the dog slobber off Marcus's face.

'I want to pee,' he whined. 'And the other.'

We'd managed in the bushes so far, but now we were in town. I asked a passing sailor where

the public toilets were. This was a new experience for Marcus. He only ever uses the toilet at home and the one at the posh baths he goes to.

We soon found it. Marcus nearly died when a woman came in with her little boy. He said, 'I can't do it in front of common people,' but he had to. When I fetched a sponge stick for him, he didn't want to touch it. I thought he was going to ask me to wipe his bottom for him, so I dumped it and left him to it.

When we'd finished, Marcus stuck out his little jaw. 'Titus, get me home,' he said. 'Now! Or you're for it.'

Halfwit. I'm for it whether I get him home now or next month.

We set off along the road out of town. I'd

expected it to be quiet, but there were plenty of travellers like us. Older, of course. Even those with mules, donkeys or carts plodded along at walking speed. Once, I heard hoof beats behind us – a messenger. I pulled Marcus out of the way. I didn't want letting him get squashed to be added to my list of crimes.

I wished we had a horse.

'Are we nearly there?' Marcus whinged.

'As we've only been walking for an hour, I doubt it,' I said. I feel sorry for him, to be honest.

He's not used to walking far, and he's certainly not used to being uncomfortable.

There was a small tavern ahead and a man was unloading wine outside it.

'Get me something to eat,' said Marcus. I felt for Aurelia's purse. Oh well.

Thank you, gods! We've got a lift, but we're not travelling with donkeys, oxen, or even horses. We're travelling with lions!

They're heading for the Roman Games, where they'll be part of a show in the amphitheatre.

Marcus is asleep. I'm bumping along on the back of a feed cart, staring straight into the face of a massive lion, the first I've ever seen. Far down the line is an elephant. I've seen them before. Our army had a great parade through the Forum once, and they had two elephants with them. I drew one for Marcus, but he said there's no such creature and slapped me for lying. Now he knows I was telling the truth!

Oh. The driver just said the menagerie train's stopping for the night. They make camp early because they have to feed the animals as well as themselves. They also have slaves (who will become gladiators in Rome) to feed and chain up for the night.

I must wake Marcus. We have to get on along the road. There are still a couple of hours of day-light left. But where will we sleep tonight?

Yesterday evening we joined on the end of a long column of soldiers who'd arrived back in Italy from Britannia. I thought we'd be safe if we stayed with them, so Marcus and I watched them build camp for the night. His little legs are worn out from keeping up with the marching men.

I didn't dare ask if we could go inside the camp, but Marcus went straight up to a guard and said, 'I am Marcus, son of Gaius Julius Felix. This is my slave, Titus, and we wish to shelter in your camp.'

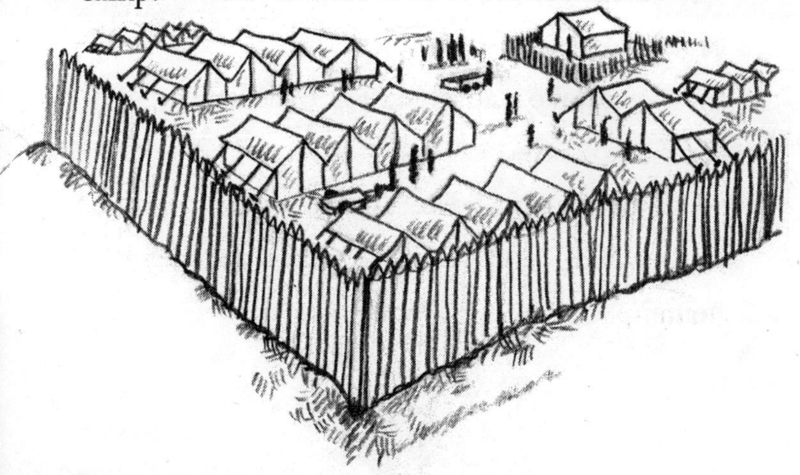

The guard laughed. 'I don't care if you're the Emperor and his pet hippopotamus,' he said. 'This is an army camp, and it's for soldiers only.'

Marcus mumbled something about, 'My father's bigger than you, and he'll get you, you wait and see,' and the soldier laughed again.

'Wait there, very important little person,' he said. In a short while he came back with two rough blankets, some bread, apples, figs and a bowl of water. 'Sleep by the gate,' he said. 'We'll keep an eye on you. You'll be safe enough.'

And we were. But when I woke, Marcus was missing. I ran around like a crazy chicken until I heard him cry out. He bobbed up from behind a bush. He'd gone for a pee and disturbed a family of hedgehogs.

'Let's take one home for Drusilla,' he said. 'Pick it up, Titus.'

I nearly exploded. 'How in the name of Jupiter am I supposed to carry a hedgehog home?'

Marcus's expression went hard, and I realised I'd gone too far. 'Sorry, Marcus,' I said. 'But it's too prickly to hold.'

'Shove it inside your tunic,' he told me, and stalked away.

I'd like to have told him where to shove it.

We've just had breakfast – bread and olives – thanks to our friendly guard, who looks worn out. It was generous of him, because soldiers have to pay for their food.

I asked him what Britannia was like. 'Gloomy and damp,' he said. I think he's made a mistake. People with golden hair like my mother must live in the sunshine.

Marcus has forgotten all about the hedgehog because he's spotted some weapons being loaded on a cart.

All I can think about is getting home today. Gaius Julius must be so angry. What will he do to me? It's terrifying to think that by this time tomorrow, I might be dead. It wasn't really my fault. I was only obeying orders.

Better get ready to move on. We've got a lift on an empty cart. The driver's on his way home from delivering wine to the docks. He said we can get a drink and food if we stop at the villa where he works. I hope so. At worst, we'll be sure to find some fruit or even just pull up a few radishes. That's if I can get I-don't-tell-lies Marcus to agree.

* * * * *

The driver didn't tell me we'd have to work for our food. I was lucky. My job was carrying manure from the stable muck heap to the vegetable beds. Poor Marcus had to help with the wine-making! He tried saying, 'Do you know who my father is?' but the farm manager just said, 'D'you want to eat or not?'

There's a lake on the farm, so when we'd finished our work, and eaten, I washed our clothes.

Then we paddled and washed ourselves. I feel better now. The pair of us are sitting stark-naked on the bank, waiting for our clothes to dry. Marcus has stopped ordering me to fetch oil and a strigil to clean his skin, and is sulking and picking at his toenails.

I've just counted Aurelia's money. There's plenty left, but that won't save my skin.

Three cartloads of wine are going to Rome this afternoon. The driver who brought us here offered us a lift. So, in two hours' time, we'll be on the last stage of our journey to Rome.

* * * * *

I'm beginning to think I'll never get Marcus home. He's a menace. I just got him dressed in his clean tunic, when he followed a dog into a walled garden. Next thing I knew, he flew back out, chased by hundreds of bees! He'd knocked a hive over.

'To the lake!' I shouted, pointing. But the idiot came straight for me! I practically yanked him off his feet and ran. We tumbled into the water, and I held him under, dragging him into

the reeds at the side. When we surfaced, we were well hidden and the bees had swarmed further along the bank. We edged off in the other direction, got out and found a sunny spot to dry off – all over again. Marcus had been stung (serves him right) and was crying. Gaius Julius would have had some herb or other to relieve the sting. I had nothing.

'Get the doctor,' Marcus sniffed.

The doctor? Huh! The first time Marcus went to the doctor's home, he was terrified by all the instruments. Gaius Julius has to pay extra to have

the doctor come to our house. Then Marcus makes a fuss and won't take his medicine (I don't blame him – it looks disgusting). Imagine if he ever had to have a tooth pulled out. Frosty-face did once, and you could hear her roars from the end of the garden. She's lucky. Gaius Julius paid for her to have a false tooth, held in place by a gold band.

I hear carts being loaded now. We must put on our damp clothes and let the sunshine – what's left of it – dry us on the way.

I don't want to get on that cart. But I know I must.

* * * * *

I don't believe it. Sometimes I think the gods don't want me to get Marcus home. There we were, trundling along, the drivers shouting rude jokes to each other. They were knocking back the wine, when our driver turned to refill his jug. The oxen plodded on, but we'd reached a bit of road that was being mended. The workmen stepped back, but one of our wheels went off the edge and over we went – oxen, cart, amphorae, driver, me – and Marcus.

I tried to catch him, but he landed with a

thump. A split second later his head cracked on a lump of stone and he tumbled into a water-filled ditch.

I cradled him in my arms. I was crying. I don't know if the tears were for Marcus or for me, because I was so afraid. There I was worrying about getting him home, and now I didn't know if he was even going to live!

Our driver was so desperate to unhitch the oxen, he didn't notice Marcus. One of the other drivers ran to a small house along the road, and fetched a woman.

'Bring him to my home,' she said. 'I'll see to him.'

She spread some horrible, smelly, greasy mixture on Marcus's bump, then laid a cold damp cloth on his forehead. A few moments later, his eyelids flickered.

I burst into tears again. Marcus will live. I prayed to all the gods at once that he would recover completely. I know that bumps on the

head can make you a bit peculiar sometimes.

I needn't have worried. The second Marcus's eyes opened he told me off for letting him fall, and demanded to know why he was wet. Back to normal.

The woman took his clothes off to dry them. Then she gave us both some bread, cheese and olives, and a cup of beer.

'Are you well enough to leave?' I asked Marcus.

'Yes, no thanks to you,' he said.

'I'll see if the driver –' I began, but the woman interrupted.

'Those carts have long gone,' she said. 'Stay and rest. You can go to Rome in the morning.'

'No!' I cried in panic. 'You don't understand! I must get Marcus home today.'

'Well, someone will be going past with fruit or veg for tomorrow's morning market,' she said. 'I'll get you a lift.'

So here we are, lying among trays of white lilies and prickly roses. The scent is wonderful.

We've stopped in a long line of traffic beside the tombs outside the city gates to wait for dusk. Then we'll be allowed in.

* * * * *

Marcus is starving. I'm too nervous to think of food. He keeps on at me to get him home, but he's not fit to walk yet. I don't want him passing out in strange streets.

'I'm scared here,' he said. 'I hate all these tombs. They're creepy.'

I don't think they're creepy. It must be nice to have your own place for ever, especially if your great achievements in life are carved on it. Like if you won a battle. I'll never have a tomb. I'll probably be cremated.

'It's getting late,' I said. 'It's too dangerous to start walking through the city. There are bad people about – thieves and murderers.'

'What about the vigiles?' he said.

The vigiles are really fire-fighters, but they also keep watch at night for criminals. Gaius Julius says there aren't enough of them, otherwise the aediles wouldn't be forever washing rude graffiti off our house.

I finally found a way to shut Marcus up. 'Someone might steal you to be a slave in some other land,' I told him.

'Don't be stupid,' he snapped.

'It happened to my mother, didn't it?'

'Of course,' he sneered, 'but she was a slave, stupid.'

'She wasn't when they took her,' I muttered (not daring to add 'stupid'). 'She was free.'

He's quiet now. The sun's almost set. It's dusk. The evening of the day I return Marcus to his family. It won't matter that I was obeying Marcus's orders when I took him into the sewer. I'll be held responsible – for everything. For him nearly drowning (because that's how Marcus will tell it), for him getting dirty and cold, having to work, being stung, being hungry, getting knocked out. I'll be responsible. I'll be punished.

I want to run! I haven't got a collar. It would be so easy to jump off this cart and never enter Rome again.

But I can't. I must take Marcus home. It's my duty. At least we're safe at the city gates now. Nothing more can go wrong.

*****

Nothing more can go wrong? How dense am I? The cart stopped at a market I'd never seen before, and the driver said, 'You're on your own now, boys. Be careful.'

It took a moment to get my bearings, then we set off. We'd walked no more than a hundred paces when we heard screams from round the corner. Marcus ran ahead to see what was happening. I chased after him, yelling, 'Come back!'

A woman was climbing out of the window of her apartment in an insula.

Two men shouted, 'Jump! We'll catch you!'

The woman jumped. Not a moment too soon, as with a whoosh! flames shot out of the windows and the whole insula went up in smoke.

'Marcus, let's get out of here,' I said. 'It's almost dark!'

'I want to watch the vigiles,' he said. 'Here they come!'

The woman suddenly screamed and ran as a

spar of wood crashed to the ground, shooting out burning splinters. Without warning, the whole upper part of the insula leaned over the street. As I grabbed Marcus round the middle and lifted him off the ground, more debris fell, sending up clouds of dust and smoke to cover us.

Clutching Marcus, I ran. 'I'm going to get you home if it's the last thing I do,' I puffed, thinking it might well be the last thing I ever did.

Once we were clear, I put Marcus down. He coughed and spluttered as he trotted along beside me. I gripped his wrist firmly. I wasn't letting go until I'd put his hand in his father's.

My determination carried me forward until we stood before our door. Then I felt as if someone had removed the bones from my legs. If I could, I'd have run. I'd have left Marcus and disappeared.

Apart from my wobbly legs, three things stopped me. The first was knowing that Gaius Julius wouldn't rest until he'd hunted me down.

The second was knowing that if he allowed me to live, I'd be punished, sold, and probably live the rest of my life in chains. Or put to death. Either way, I'd never see Britannia. The third thing that stopped me was Marcus hammering on the door, bellowing, 'It's me and Titus. Let us in!'

When Damon flung the door open, Marcus completely disappeared in a swirl of arms and legs and togas and stolas. I got slobbered on by Ferox.

The family swooped Marcus into the atrium, then set him down and fussed over him and

brushed dirt off him. Drusilla spat on a corner of her tunic and wiped his smutty face, tears pouring from her eyes.

I stayed where I was. I didn't know what to do.

After a few moments, Gaius Julius turned to me. 'Come in, Titus.'

I slid inside. The door closed behind me.

'Come here,' said Gaius Julius.

I obeyed, bracing myself for the blow that was about to hit me.

But instead of striking me, my master's hands went to my shoulders. He tipped up my chin.

'Open your eyes, Titus.'

I did. He looked at me sternly.

'I cannot judge until I know what's happened,' he said. 'All I do know is that my son has come home. For that I am grateful. He'll be bathed and put to bed, and I will send for a doctor to make sure he's all right.'

I started to sob. I don't know why. It was just

all too much, and I couldn't believe Gaius Julius wasn't beating me. At least, not yet.

'Go to bed, Titus,' he continued. 'Tomorrow we will talk.'

Milla brought me some bread and meat and beer. She hugged me! 'I'm glad to see you,' she said. 'We slaves have been so worried about you, Titus. We knew something terrible had happened.'

Worried about me! She didn't mention Marcus. Just me! That made me cry again.

When Milla had gone, I climbed out of bed and fetched my treasure box. It's all I own. It isn't much.

* * * * *

I felt better this morning until Gaius Julius sent for me. He was wearing a tunic, which meant there'd be no callers.

'Titus,' he began, 'I've heard Marcus's story. Tell me yours.'

I told him the truth. Why I was in the sewer. My treasure box. The freedom fund. The things I did wrong. The things I did right. The whole truth. When I'd finished, he said, 'What do you think I should do with you?'

I bit my lip. I didn't want to put ideas in his head like beatings or execution if they weren't already there. 'Sell me?' I suggested. It seemed safest.

Gaius Julius put out his hand – and ruffled my hair! He burst out laughing!

'Sell you? Sell the slave who might have run away to escape punishment and left my son to be eaten by bears or wolves? No, Titus, I won't sell you.'

I was so relieved I nearly sat down – in front of my master!

He called Marcus in. 'From now on,' he said to him, 'Titus will obey you, of course. But if he ever thinks that obeying an order will lead you into danger, he will first ask another member of the family what he should do. Do you understand that, Marcus?'

'Yes, Father.'

'Titus?'

'Yes, master. Thank you, master.'

Then Gaius Julius opened a box and took out a coin. It was a copper as.

He held out the coin. Marcus went to take it, but Gaius Julius said, 'It's not for you. It's for Titus.'

'Me?'

'For your treasure box.'

Then Gaius Julius made me a promise. As long as I stay loyal to the family, and am a good, obedient slave, he will give me one of these coins every seven days towards my freedom fund.

I couldn't speak.

'You will have to add your own share when you can,' said my master. 'As you get older and more experienced, you will help look after our guests. If you please them, they will no doubt reward you. Off you go, now. Back to work.'

We left the tablinum, and I headed for the kitchen.

'Titus.'

I looked back. Marcus was poking an uneven tile with his toe.

'You don't have to save money in your treasure box,' he said, as he stamped the tile back into place (and cracked it). 'When I'm grown up, I'll give you your freedom!'

I clutched my coin. I've got far more faith in my treasure box than in Marcus. I turned towards the kitchen and – whoops! Straight over Ferox! It wasn't a jug of liquamen that went into the impluvium this time – it was my coin.

That's how my master, who last saw me standing before him in gratitude, came upon me on my hands and knees, groping in the household water supply. 'Titus?'

'Sorry, Master. I tripped over Ferox, and now I feel funny.' I did too.

Milla peered at me when I reached the kitchen. 'You don't look yourself at all, Titus.'

'I don't feel myself,' I said. And I didn't. Later, as I went to put my coin away, I thought how glad I am to feel safe again. I've seen how horrible life is for some slaves. But I'm lucky. This is my home. And I will be free one day.

I'll see Britannia, I know I will. But in the meantime, I can be happy here in Rome – above ground. I never want to smell the inside of a sewer ever again!

Toby lifted his head carefully. He didn't want to make himself dizzy again. 'A coin of my own,' he murmured. 'A coin to help make me free –'

He looked round. Fairies! He was back!

'Whew! I'm me again,' he said. 'I'm Toby Tucker. But I was Titus. And I saved Marcus, and one day Titus will be – was! – free.'

He looked at the wooden chest. How come something so ordinary-looking had such extraordinary power?

Toby thought of all the scraps of names inside it. 'So much more to learn about my family,' he murmured.

Hearing a noise outside, he went to the window. Don was loading boxes in the car. Toby remembered saying he'd help. That was – how long ago?

'Centuries!' he chuckled, as he ran downstairs. On the way outside, he passed Evie, who was flat out on the sofa enjoying a cup of tea and half an hour with her book. For a split second, he

felt the urge to tell her of the amazing things that happened to him. But something stopped him.

I don't really know you well enough, Toby thought. Not yet.

He and Don loaded the car with all the bits Evie had decided they didn't need – lampshades, odd pieces of china, ancient tools and several ornaments no one could find a home for.

'Here.' Don held out a mauve spotted china toadstool. 'This would look nice in your room.'

Toby looked puzzled. 'Eh?'

'Somewhere for all those fairies to sit!'

Toby pretended to punch Don. Then he said, 'I've been thinking. I'm going to start saving. I thought it would take too long to get anything good, but it doesn't matter how long, does it?'

'I always say,' said Don, 'if a thing's worth having, it's worth waiting for.'

Toby thought of how Titus was going to save for years and years for what he wanted. Surely he could save for a few months to get a second-hand bike. Or maybe a new game to play on Jake's console thingy? Or maybe a games console of his own!

Once the car was loaded, they went back in.

'Isn't it dinner time?' Don asked.

Evie groaned, got up and followed them into the kitchen. 'Chicken casserole. OK?'

Don examined the pudding. 'What's this?' He poked it. 'Cement?'

Toby waited.

Evie spooned up a chunk of tinned pear and

flicked it at Don. It got him – splat – on the forehead. 'It's a beautiful meringue, and you're not having any!'

Toby laughed. 'More for me!'

While they were eating, Evie asked if Toby had had any more luck with the family tree.

He nodded. 'I found the name "Titus",' he said. 'He was a slave in Ancient Rome.'

'How do you know he was a slave?' asked Don.

'Just do,' said Toby, getting up to fetch the meringue. 'Wow! This weighs a ton!'

'To-beee!' Evie growled.

He laughed. 'Just joking.'

She looked at him. 'You're always bright and lively after a session with your family tree.'

He grinned. 'One day I'll tell you why.'

Maybe next time, he thought. Because there would be a next time. He was sure of it. But what time?

TOBY TUCKER

be next?

He's Seti, keeping sneaky secrets in Ancient Egypt!

TOBY TUCKER
Dodging the Donkey Doo
VAL WILDING

He's Niko, dodging the donkey doo in Ancient Greece!

Sydenham Community library

Phone 0208 778 1753
www.lewisham.gov.uk/myservices/libraries

Borrowing

Patron	Master Ashwath Nivas
Patron ID	0150004[illegible]

		Due Date
1	Asterix and the [illegible] Goscinny and Uderzo	26/01/15
2	Asterix and the secret weapon	26/01/15
3	Sludging through a sewer	26/01/15

05.01.2015 12:54:01

Thank you and see you soon

He's John Bunn, mucking about with monkeys in Tudor London!

He's Alfie Trott, picking people's pockets in Victorian London!

He's Fred Barrow, hogging all the pig swill in wartime London!

EGMONT PRESS: ETHICAL PUBLISHING

Egmont Press is about turning writers into successful authors and children into passionate readers – producing books that enrich and entertain. As a responsible children's publisher, we go even further, considering the world in which our consumers are growing up.

Safety First
Naturally, all of our books meet legal safety requirements. But we go further than this; every book with play value is tested to the highest standards – if it fails, it's back to the drawing-board.

Made Fairly
We are working to ensure that the workers involved in our supply chain – the people that make our books – are treated with fairness and respect.

Responsible Forestry
We are committed to ensuring all our papers come from environmentally and socially responsible forest sources.

For more information, please visit our website at
www.egmont.co.uk/ethicalpublishing

Egmont
Press
is committed to
Ethical
Publishing
www.egmont.co.uk/ethicalpublishing